Criminally Bound

MAUREEN SHIGENO

CRIMINALLY BOUND

Maureen Shigeno

Credits:

Cover Design/Interior Formatting: CPR Publishing Services

Editor: Abby Formatting & Content Editing & Web Design

Proofreader: CPR Publishing Services

DISCLAIMER: This book includes explicit scenes. It is intended for readers 18+.

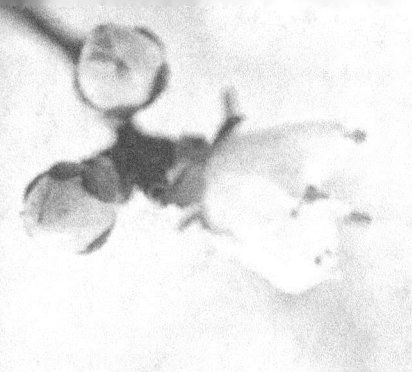

THIS BOOK IS DEDICATED TO MY MANY
LOYAL AND WONDERFUL READERS.

YOU'RE THE REASON I HAVE THE
STRENGTH TO KEEP WRITING.

THANK YOU SO MUCH.

One

EMIKA

The knots in my stomach twist tighter.

I shouldn't have eaten dinner. I feel sick. Hell, I've felt sick for days, but it only gets worse as the time of the announcement grows closer. Now I'm just waiting for the bomb to drop.

I'm sitting in the large dining area we use to throw parties. The place screams wealth, and I am dolled up to play my part. As the only daughter of a popular yakuza boss, I've been given a lot in life. Opportunities aren't one of them.

I'm considered a nuisance to my stepmother. I'm the byproduct of one of my father's flings. He has a lot, but I'm the only child from them. Since my older brother is the child of my father and his wife, he's like a prince in my stepmother's eyes, while I'm just someone she should tolerate for fear of my

5

father's rage.

As a yakuza boss, my father is powerful, and with power comes greed. I don't think there has ever been a time he hasn't cheated on his wife. My stepmother doesn't seem to mind. She even hangs out with most of his mistresses—just never with my mother. Mom's an outcast, a vacationer from America. It seems she only stayed long enough to make me and give birth. I think she could have kept me, but she would've had to stay— and apparently leaving was more important than me.

I've been unwanted from the start. By my mother and by everyone else in my family.

Until him.

Peering through my eyelashes, I glance across the room. At him. Kade. That hulk of a man is gorgeous in a suit. He's hot as hell in anything, but I rarely see him in a suit since suits are reserved for the upper men in the family business. He's hired muscle for the yakuza group my father runs. Lower down the chain, but there's awestruck chatter of how fast he's moving up in the family business.

Kade was discovered in an underground fight my father was hosting six months ago. He's always looking for recruits, and Kade seemed to get his praise, because Dad's been keeping him around ever since.

The first time I saw him, I was mesmerized. With his powerful and strong figure, he was intimidating at first, but there was also a part of me that couldn't stop admiring him.

Like now. I can't take my eyes away from him. He stands out, not only because he's not Japanese, but because of how good-looking he is. He's over six and a half feet tall with green eyes and an imposing form. Most men around here are lean, but he's hard and ripped all over. Deliciously so.

I would know. I've been sneaking into his room for the past two months. He doesn't know it's me. I never let him turn the lights on. That's my dirty little secret. One I'll cherish for the rest of my life.

Rarely do newcomers stay at our house, but when employees have nowhere else to go, my father likes to show he's a good person by being hospitable. If my father only knew what I've been up to at night, under his roof…

I shake the thoughts away. Even the fear of him can't stop me from chasing that high whenever I'm with Kade.

He's a table away from where I'm seated with my family and all the important people in the business. But I can still tell his voice apart from the others through the crowd. It's amazing how well he speaks Japanese.

I watch his mouth move sensually. God, his lips are ripe with color against his facial hair. So juicy. Perfect for biting. And that's one of my favorite things to do whenever I get the chance to be in his arms.

He's the freedom in my somewhat sheltered life.

Unless you're a member of the yakuza, people are afraid of you. I've been trained since day one on how to be the perfect wife. The only part I have rebelled against is my virginity. I had to give it to him. I had to have that slice of freedom. I had to have *him*.

Since I was a child, I've known my marriage would be a loveless one. I knew not to keep my hopes up from an early age. I'm just a bargaining chip for my father to grow his empire. I'll be married to whoever he sees fit, and my virginity will be the prize.

But this time, I chose the winner.

Kade certainly enjoyed it.

We've been together almost every night since that first one. I sneak out in the middle of the night after he falls asleep, leaving him behind. I want to spend all night in his arms, I want to wake up with him, but I can't risk it. If anyone catches us, we'll both be dead. Without my virginity, my only use to my father will be as a whore for the men to pass around. There are a lot of those hanging around as well.

Surveying the room of formal attire and spiffy staff members, I note how close we are getting to my father's next speech. He always gives one at the beginning of dinner at these functions he hosts once a month. Occasionally, he announces something great that has happened to a member of the yakuza. This time, it will be about me.

I can't help but wonder what Kade will think when he finds out. Probably nothing. I'm just another kid to him in the light of the day. I can't say I blame him.

I am his boss's daughter and at least twenty years younger than he is. I don't know his actual age, but judging by the wrinkles around his mouth and eyes when he smiles or laughs, it's a big difference. Why would he even care what happens to me? He doesn't know me. He knows the woman he spends his nights with.

He only acknowledges me when he has no way of avoiding me, like around others. He doesn't even say "hello" when we pass each other in the hall. He keeps his distance and he never looks or accidentally brushes against me. He walks right by me as if I'm invisible. In the daylight, I am.

I sigh. My back stiffens as the waiters take away our plates and replace them with mini personal cakes. It's so cute—white angel cakes covered in whipped icing and strawberries on top. I cringe at the tiny rectangular piece of chocolate with the word 'congratulations' written decoratively in white sitting with the fruit.

Here it comes…

As soon as the waiters are done and standing by the wall with their hands cupped in front of them, my father stands. Lean, tall—although not as tall as Kade—and powerful. It radiates off him like a beacon of honor in his crisp white suit. But tonight, he'll use that power to decide my fate.

I want to throw up.

The room grows silent, and everyone's eyes are on him. Down the table is my husband-to-be. He's my half-brother's second; if my brother should die after he inherits the family business, he'll get everything.

To anyone else, Kenji is a great choice for me. He's only eight years older than me, has been a part of the business for a decade, and is well-respected. But he's a dick. Not a normal dick either. A *dick* dick. You know, the kind that has no morals.

From the yakuza women, who have their own type of gang, I've heard so many secrets about the people around me. And I've heard the rumors about Kenji—enough to know he's not nice. He likes to throw his weight around. Catch my drift?

He's not someone you want to be tied to forever. Yet I have no choice.

My father claps his hands, as if he needs to get everyone's attention. I roll my eyes at his theatrics. He spreads his arms with an enormous smile on his face. At my father's nod, Kenji stands, proud and beaming.

Then he looks at me.

I want to run.

I want to scream.

I *really* want to run screaming!

Instead, I stand. Back straight, eyes focused on the far wall. I can't face these people. I don't want to see the satisfied smile on my stepmother's face. It's been a week since my father told us I'm to be married. I've been miserable, while my stepmother has been in a great mood.

One week. That's how long it's been since I visited Kade's room. It's the longest I've gone without being with him since we started this twisted game of sexy nightcaps. And now I want to look at him for support, but I can't face him knowing what I know.

I want to be with him so badly. I know I'll tell him who I am and beg him to save me the second we're alone. But I can't risk it. I can't ruin our perfect memories with haunted ones of him telling me to leave and the look of disgust that will transform his sexy face.

"As you all know, we recently celebrated my daughter's twenty-first birthday." My father motions over to me with a proud smile.

I force myself to smile back, blinking away tears. He speaks again to the room. I move my eyes back to the wall. I can feel eyes on me. I want to look around to see who dares to watch me while my father is speaking, but I don't. I need all the strength I can muster to keep my head held high. Otherwise, my father will punish me for embarrassing him during such an important moment.

Trust me, I know. He's done it before. The tattoo on my back only covers some of the scars.

"I'd like to announce another wonderful occasion with you all tonight," my father says. "Kenji and Emika are engaged to be married, and after much deliberation, we've decided to have the wedding next weekend."

My eyes widen at this new development. He's already set a date?

Of course the old bastard has. And in a week!

In their eyes, I only need to know what will happen. Details are not important, because as a woman, I'm rated below them. My job is to sit back, support my husband, cook, clean, and take care of his every need…all while looking great doing it.

Sexist pigs. All of them!

Applause lights up the room. My father bows and thanks them as if it's all about him.

I guess, technically, it is. Damn sure isn't about me.

Two

KADE

What the fuck just happened?

I seem to be asking myself that a lot lately. Along with *what the fuck am I doing?*

Six months ago, my life was clear. I knew what I was doing here. I knew what I needed to do to infiltrate this yakuza crime family. I have clear instructions: get in, free the girls they are selling, kill the members, and get out.

See? Easy as shit.

Not really.

For the first time in my entire career as a hitman, I have gotten sidetracked. It's *her* fault. With her sexy dark hair, sexy dark eyes, sexy fucking everything!

God damn it!

The second I laid eyes on her, my dick went hard, my mind

stopped working, and I was a goner.

I don't just want her body. No, I need to have *her*. Have everything. That is something I've never felt before. Getting laid has never been my problem. Even around here, I can have my pick of ass.

But no, my dick has to point to the one thing I can't have. Of course, that only makes me want it more.

Stop fucking judging me. I can hear it. Yes, she's far too young for me, and yes, I know I should keep my distance.

And I do. During the day.

But when she comes crawling into my bed at night, I can't say no. I need her like I need air to breathe. I've known who she is since the first night she came to me. Her scent of cherry blossoms wafted over as she hesitantly stood beside my bed that first night.

Contemplating the smartness of her plan, probably. I bet she thought I was asleep.

I wasn't. I'm never asleep when she comes. I just pretend to be.

Living the life I do, being alert and ready for anything is a force of habit. Nothing gets by me. Not a sound down the hall, not a flicker of light outside my window. And definitely not her delicious scent or the gorgeous outline of her body.

I'm built for stealth. And murder. That's my job. Have I mentioned I'm good at it?

Fifteen years as a Navy SEAL and five as a contract killer. Killing is my life, and I've never fucked up a job. Never gotten distracted.

Except on this one. The one where she climbs in my bed each night. Hell, I don't even realize I'm holding my breath every time she comes into the room until she gets in the bed with me. When it comes to her, I'm like a lovesick puppy.

And I'm in my fucking forties!

Do you know how much concentration and self-control it takes not to look at her when I feel her nearby, or when she walks by me? Do you have any idea how hard I have to fight the urge to grab her and take her on the nearest hard surface?

It's not for pansies, let me tell you.

And this last week has been driving me up a wall!

My body yearns for her; I'm going to explode if I don't get inside her soon. I lie awake at night, wondering what I did to scare her off. Then, during the daylight—when I can get out some frustrations by pounding shitheads—I revel in it, but nothing eases the hunger I feel for her. She has me wrapped around her little fucking finger so tight, and she doesn't even know it.

No woman has ever gotten to me like she has. She has me thinking about crazy shit, like how I'm going to tell her I've come to take down her family, and how I'm going to keep her out of this mess. I've even thought about waking up next to her every day and shit.

I've never wanted or even considered things like marriage and a baby. I never wanted a family. Mine is bad enough to teach me to never have one. The only time it was quiet and peaceful was when my parents ignored each other instead of fighting. No way in hell do I want to punish an innocent kid with that kind of fucked-up shit. I wouldn't know what to do with a kid, let alone raise one. Same thing with a wife.

But with her, I can't stop thinking about those things. The idea of her pregnant with my baby does things to me I can't explain.

What the hell is wrong with me?

I'm not one to settle. I get bored easily, and that's why this job is perfect for me. I can be one person long enough to finish the job, and when it's over, I change to someone else. No attachments. No ties. I don't even have a place to call home. My few things are in a storage unit in California.

I'm free as a bird. Or I used to be.

Not anymore.

Emika makes me want to be someone I've never been before. Someone who normally makes me want to run away.

But I want it with her. *For* her.

She deserves so much more than a criminal life. Her personality doesn't fit in any of this. She radiates white picket fences and wrap-around porches.

Now I'm seeing she'll never get it, even if I try to change my life around.

Her father, Ren, is a piece of work. I've met my fair share of assholes, but he takes the cake. Literally. If he wants something, he'll do whatever it takes to get it—including human trafficking. He's been a pain in the ass for Japan for years. It was when he started expanding into the U.S. that he got on my client's radar. Kidnapping the daughter of a senator is not the smartest play. Even for Ren.

The senator was so furious he refused to work with the police. He wanted revenge, and that's why he came looking for me. He found my number from some seedy places I no longer step into. Not that I'm afraid, I'm just not in the mood to hang out down there anymore. I've moved up, but my name is tossed around a lot as if I'm a god.

You won't hear me complaining. My praise is what gets me the high-paying jobs. And I must admit, I enjoy playing with my prey. Hence the unhurried attitude I have for this undercover op I'm doing. I need Ren to trust me so he'll tell me where the girls are, and then I can watch the fear creep into his eyes as I kill him. The moment when he least expects it.

But this new announcement has me pulled in two directions. I don't think I have that much time anymore.

Unable to stop myself, I look over at Emika. She's not paying attention to me. Her eyes are fixed on a far wall with a look of determined pride. She looks beautiful in her flowy white dress, like a goddess. The look of innocence and pliability is what they are probably going for, but as I know how wild she gets in the bedroom, I know she's anything but those things.

A smirk curves my lips. I'd love to see the rage on Kenji's face when I tell him she's mine. That I have taken what he's most looking forward to. I want to pound my fist into his face until he stops breathing for even thinking he has a chance with Emika. Sick shit.

But I can't do those things if I don't want to blow my cover. I have to remember my cover. It's not just about the money. It's about those poor girls who don't deserve to be taken and treated like cattle.

I love killing, but I only kill and take jobs that fit me. And this one does. Taking out a nasty son of a bitch like Ren, along with others in the business, will be a pleasure.

I focus back on Emika. Why won't she look at me?

She smiles like she's supposed to at the applause, as if she's happy, but I've never seen a real twinkling smile on her face. Maybe she doesn't know how to be happy. There's always something dark hidden behind her eyes. Some hidden story buried deep within, proving how little emotional support she's had in her life.

She deserves to be happy. I want to give that happiness to

her. For some strange reason, I want to be her hero.

Well, as much of one as I can be.

I'm not sure she'll want me once she finds out the truth about who I really am, so I'll wait on that tidbit, but I do know it's time to tell her I know she's my sexy nightingale. No more acting like strangers.

Also, I need to find where they hid the girls soon, because as much as I want to save Emika from this life, I can't leave those innocent little girls to fend for themselves.

I focus back on Ren's speech. After he explains the details about where and when the glorious occasion will happen—his way of personally inviting everyone—we all applaud again and go back to dessert. I take a few bites, chat with my colleagues, and play the all-around great badass I'm supposed to be, but shit is sitting in my stomach like goddamn gumballs.

I keep watching Emika out the corner of my eye. The minute the meal is concluded, and people start moving around the room, mostly to congratulate the groom and father of the bride, she slinks off. I knew she would. She has never liked these events, but stays to appease her father. She usually stays longer, though. Proving she's more miserable with the marriage than she's letting on.

I make my way toward Kenji and the boss. They're laughing and shaking hands with other mindless fucks, but I'm not staying here, and I have to speak to him before I leave or I'll screw up everything I've been working for during the last six months. It's time to speed things up.

Like the asshole I'm supposed to be, I walk right up to them and interrupt. 'Cause what else would Kade Donovan do?

"Oyabun," I say in a booming voice filled with mirth.

Ren turns to look at me with a scowl on his face, but his

smile quickly returns when he sees it's me. This asshat loves me. Dumbass.

"Kade-san!" He reaches out to shake my hand. "I'm so glad you could make it tonight."

I roll my eyes internally.

On the outside, I paste on a fake smile. "Congratulations on the upcoming nuptials. There is no one better than Kenji-san."

He pats Kenji on the back with pride. "Just as I said. What did I tell you, Kenji? Kade-san has an eye for things."

And, just like that, he's eating out of the palm of my hand again.

Kenji smiles, chuckling as he shakes my hand next. "It's good to see you again. Thank you for your support."

He's so full of shit. He hates me. For an idiot, he's pretty good at reading people. Not as good as me, because I'd be dead if he was, but he's suspicious of how fast I'm moving up in the boss's good graces. If it wouldn't have raised too many eyebrows, I'd have killed him the first chance I got—and there have been several. But he's important to the boss and well-known, so he gets to live.

For now. Damn it.

We chat for a few more minutes, shooting the shit with a few other people who come around, and the moment I get the chance, I sneak out of the room without any problem.

Ten fucking minutes is a lifetime when your girl's waiting for you.

Three

EMIKA

Sighing again, I throw myself back on the bed with my arms spread wide. What the hell am I going to do? At least, no one has come knocking on my door to check on me, so they haven't noticed my earlier-than-usual escape. Too busy taking credit for my wedding, no doubt.

I'm relieved, really, but being alone is not always great. I wish I had someone to talk to, to vent my pain to…

When someone barges into my room, I hurry back to my feet and smooth out my dress.

"I was coming back." I rush to explain my absence. "I just needed a sec—"

My words are cut off in a gasp when someone wraps an arm around my waist, whirls me around to slam into a hard wall of muscular chest, and takes my mouth in a rough, open-mouthed kiss. I instantly melt into the familiar taste and feeling of Kade. His tongue duels with mine; our teeth knock together. My fingers curl into biceps that are bigger than my thighs and a moan spills into his mouth from my own.

God, I'll never get over how good it feels being with him. He tastes of sake and his own personal flavor that always makes me wetter than the ripest peach. He releases his own growl of approval, biting my lip and sucking it into his mouth. With a pop, he lets it go and buries his nose in my neck.

He inhales deeply. "Fuck, I miss the smell of you on my sheets."

"You…you knew?" I stammer.

Between his body pressing into mine and that kiss, my mouth can't seem to catch up with my brain.

Leaning back, he gives me a sultry smile. "Nothing gets by me."

He straightens, loosening his grip on my waist. I have to crane my neck back to look into his eyes. Seriously, he's a giant compared to my five feet. I've never really been able to see what it would be like standing together since we've always been horizontal, but damn. We would be a sight. Skyscraper versus Thumbelina.

Blushing, I dip my head. I wish my hair was down and not tied in this fucking bun so I could hide my face better. Curling a thick digit under my chin, Kade lifts my eyes back to his as he crouches down a bit, still smirking like the cocky prick he is.

"You have a severe hiding problem. You're going to have to stop that shit."

I shrug, letting my eyes avoid his. My flushed skin only gets warmer. "I didn't think you'd want me if you knew."

"Why?" His dark voice holds amusement.

"Because we're not exactly on the same level, if you know what I mean."

"Age?"

"Yes." I frown up at him. "Doesn't it bother you?"

Pecking my lips gently, he says, "Not really. I've been around long enough to realize shit doesn't always happen according to plan. I've learned to just go with the flow and wing it."

"People say things."

"People talk shit either way," he says. "But if you have a problem with that, then you'd better say something now."

A smirk curves my lips. "And if I don't?"

"Then buckle up, woman, because this is going to be a bumpy ride."

I gasp as he grips my ass in his big hands and lifts me. Wrapping my legs around his waist, I curl my fingers into his hair and pull his lips to mine.

I can't believe he wants me. *Me.* A woman with no experience except for what we've done together, and someone way below his league. He could have anyone, but he wants me.

I'm done running away. A week without him is not something I'll choose to do ever again. He knows my secrets. He sees me, and he's still here. No way am I going to let that gift go. I'm going to show him just how much I need him.

Everyone else is busy with the party. They won't hear a thing, and I need him too much to care. Biting his bottom lip, I tug until he hisses, his fingers digging deeper into my ass cheeks. I barely register his movements until I'm tossed on the bed.

With a gasp, I bounce on the mattress. The growl that leaves his throat as he roughly removes his suit jacket has my cheeks flushing for a whole different reason. Seeing him so out of control—for *me*—makes me crazy with need. My panties are already soaked.

Leaning up on my elbows, I lick my lips. His green eyes darken as he stares down at me like a starved man. He probably is. I know I'm going to die if he doesn't do something soon.

He loosens his tie enough to pull it over his head and drops it to the floor carelessly alongside his jacket. I watch with heavy-lidded eyes as his tattooed fingers grip the collar of his shirt.

A shudder runs through my body as the sound of fabric ripping fills the room. Fuck. He's delicious. I drink in the view of him. Muscles stacked on muscles and covered in black and white tattoos gleaming back at me.

Unable to resist, I sit up and crawl across the bed toward him, my gaze locking with his. My hands are the first to reach him. Yanking roughly at the belt on his black slacks, I purr up at him as his hand caresses over the elegant high, textured chignon my hair is pulled into. A sexy, deviant smirk curves his lips as he watches me.

Getting the belt open, I immediately move on to his pants and shove them down. A moan leaves my lips at the sight of his dick springing free. God, it's beautiful. My mouth waters at the swollen, veiny cock. I don't have any experience with men other than Kade, so I have nothing to compare it to, but it must be larger than normal—at least ten inches long, and not skinny either. The damn thing looks like a mushroom-headed rod of steel, and it's usually ramming into me. My pussy clenches at the thought.

Wrapping my hand around his cock, I stroke it slowly, watching his reaction. A feeling of power races through me at the sight of this enormous man closing his eyes, head falling back on a groan of pleasure. Leaning forward and opening my mouth, I look up at him through my eyelashes.

His hand tightens in my hair for a second as I suck him into the back of my throat and pull back up to the tip—just the way he taught me he likes it—before his hooded eyes come back into view to watch my mouth slide as far over him as I can go. As I said, he's hung. Even with me opening my throat, I can't fit all of him inside. My hand moves in sync with my mouth to make up for what it misses.

"That's my girl," he coos, smoothing his palm over my hair. "Sexy little vixen. You love sucking my big cock, don't you?"

I hum my approval as I keep slurping and bobbing my head on him. My movements get faster with my excitement.

"God, you have the perfect mouth." His words trail off on a groan and his eyes close. "I've missed fucking you. Jacking off to thoughts of you is not nearly enough to satisfy me. I'm going to come down that pretty little throat, and you're going to swallow all of it, understand?"

I nod the best I can, digging my nails into his thigh for more stability while my other hand and mouth move faster over his cock. I want to taste him again. I need that salty-sweet flavor coating my tongue. His body tenses and his fingers curl into my bun. He's close—so fucking close—and I'm dripping between my legs knowing what's to come.

As much as he's missed me, I've been dying inside every second he hasn't been with me. I love seeing his bare body lusting for mine in the lighting of my room. We've always done it in the dark, but there are no more secrets between us. He accepts me, and I can do nothing but surrender to this hulking hunk of a man.

When he comes, he throws his head back, thrusts into my

mouth, and growls my name. I swallow around his length, pulling more from him, and close my eyes, savoring his essence.

God, he's turned me into a nymphomaniac. And I love it.

Kade's fingers loosen, and I slowly suck his dick clean. I lick my lips and smile up at him. The dazed look on his face tells me I have done well. All too soon, that predatory gleam is back in his eyes, and I can't say I'm disappointed to see it.

He pushes me back with a hand on my shoulder. "My turn."

I lie back and let my legs fall open. Kade shoves my skirt up to my waist, out of his way, and rips my white panties on a grunt, diving right in. I can't help the cry that leaves me. He's sucking, nipping, and flicking that damn thick tongue of his, all the while growling and hooking his arms around my legs to stop my squirming. The pleasure is overwhelming with his demanding tongue.

Fuck.

It's so much all at once that it doesn't take long for my orgasm to crash through me like a tidal wave. I'm so lost, I can't think enough to stifle the screams of pleasure he's eliciting from me.

Four

KADE

Emika's sweet juices flow down my throat and cover my facial scruff. I revel in it. Another groan rumbles from my chest as I eat her pussy through her orgasm. Her body quivers, her hips rock as far as my arms will let her, and when she finishes riding out her pleasure, her body deflates to the mattress under us.

I don't even care that she screamed the house down. She's always so careful not to make too much noise, but she's let her inhibitions go this time. I love it. Plus, with the party downstairs, no one will hear. They're all so drunk and high off the strip show that always happens after dinner that a stampede of elephants could come through and they wouldn't notice.

These are the perfect nights to use as a cover for their massacre once I find the girls they've been black-marketing, but they only happen once a month, and I no longer have a month to finish my job.

And I'm damn sure not waiting for that fucking wedding to happen.

Shaking off the thought before I ruin the hard cock I have for Emika, I wipe my mouth with my hand and lift up on my knees. Gripping her waist, I lean back and flip her onto her stomach. She's so much smaller than me, I could probably hurt her if I wasn't careful, but she never complains. She takes whatever I give her with hunger that matches my own.

And our size difference makes the sex even better.

Emika lies there, lax and sedated. She's still recovering from her orgasm, but I know she will be ready for me. She always is.

I put my hands at the top of her dress on either side of the zipper and yank with a growl of triumph. The silky fabric rips perfectly down the middle. Her naked back is exposed to me, and I run my fingers over the scars I've felt many times. She shivers at my touch, but doesn't stop me. She usually shies away when I feel them in the dark until I smack her ass and demand her to stay still. She always complies and eventually relaxes against me, but this time, I don't have to do anything to make her remain where she is. She's too far gone to care, or maybe she finally trusts me.

The scars vary between small circular burns and slight cut marks. They aren't big, but they're numerous. The tattoo on her back of a snake wrapped in vines has me curious, but I don't dare ask her about it now.

Soon. I'll learn her every secret soon.

Slapping her ass to watch it jiggle and turn red, I rasp, "On your knees."

She pulls her legs up to bend at the knees, but keeps her

head down. Good girl. She has learned what I want quickly and she's always so obedient. My dick jerks, ready to feel her tight pussy wrapped around it again.

I get off the bed long enough to grab a condom out of the wallet in my pants and slip it on. I smack her ass again on the other cheek for good measure as I get back into position behind her. Her back arches, and she wiggles that round ass at me. Gripping the base of my cock, I hold onto her hip with my other hand and rub the head over her pussy, coating it with her juices. She moans and moves against me, pressing more onto my dick as I rub it against her. She's well over her climax and ready to go again.

I smile. She's always ready for me. I love it. It makes me feel like a king. *Her* king.

Moving a little closer, I still her movements, and she arches her ass higher to give me even better access to her dripping wet pussy. I'm not a small man, so I always make sure she's more than ready for me before I take her.

I slip the tip of my dick into her entrance. She's so wet, it slips in past the head with little effort. When I feel a bit of resistance, I pull back and slowly rock back in. It takes a few tries since we haven't been together in a week and her pussy is naturally tight as fuck, but when my pelvis finally hits her ass, we both sigh at the feeling of being one again.

"Fuck, I've missed this pussy," I hiss, pulling out slowly and slamming back in.

Her body rocks from the force, but she pushes back against me, taking what I give like the good girl she is. One hand on the small of her back, I tug at the destroyed updo that pools at her waist as I shove my dick in and out of her, setting a rhythm that's hard and fast. Her head is pulled back, cries of pleasure leaving her luscious mouth.

We've had slow sex, hard sex, teasing sex, and almost everything in between, and yet I can never get enough of her. A lifetime won't be enough. Deep down, I know that. She's mine. No matter what anyone else says. I'll keep her and kill anyone who tries to take her from me.

The thought just makes me fuck her harder, sweat beading on my brow from the exertion. She doesn't mind. She's moaning, thrusting her body into the rhythm I've set.

Fuck, I love this woman. I'm not sure when it happened, but damn if it isn't true, and I couldn't care less.

"Mine," I growl, spanking her. "Say it."

"Yours! Oh God, Kade! Yes!"

Reaching under her, I rub her clit in circles. "Are you going to come for me, baby girl?"

"K...ade..." She gasps between breaths.

The walls of her pussy tighten on my shaft. She's so close, and thank God, because I'm losing control over my own orgasm. She feels too damn good. Fuck.

"Don't come until I tell you to."

Emika tenses, trying to hold back. I smile at how well she listens to me. I keep up the fast, rough pace, loving the way she struggles. She only lasts another minute before she's begging.

"Oh, God...ahh...baby...yes... I need to come... Please..." she whimpers.

Sweat is coating both of our skin. Leaning down, I lick a line up her spine to her neck. Emika turns her head to me, and I oblige her and kiss her, letting our tongues dance in a mind-blowing duel that matches the rhythm of our hips. Wrapping a hand around her throat, I lean back on my knees, pulling her up with me so her back is pressed to my front. I release her mouth and watch the dazed, wild look in her dark eyes. Her lips are swollen from my kiss and parted as she gasps for breath.

I move my hand from her hips to between her legs and start strumming her clit while I pound the shit out of her pussy. I tighten my grip on her throat just enough to thrill her, but not enough to cut off her airflow, and growl into her ear.

"Come. Now."

I pinch her clit. The pleasure-pain sets her off. Her pussy pulses, drawing out my seed. Her screams mingle in the room with my roar as I pump into her a few more times and still on my release.

As I relax my grip on her, she slumps to the bed, completely wrecked from our games. My dick slips from her, and I can't help gripping it and giving it a few more tugs, loving the feeling of her juices.

Fuck, I hate condoms. One day, we're going to stop using them, and she'll be barefoot and pregnant all the time.

I catch my breath and climb off the bed. I open a door, but it's the walk-in closet. Damn, she has a lot of shit. Moving on, I open another door on the back wall. Finally, I find the en-suite and go in search of the washcloths. After tossing the used condom into the trash, I clean off my dick. Fucker's still half-cocked. If I didn't have to work, I'd climb back into bed with her and take her again.

It will have to wait. Damn it.

I grab a clean washcloth and wet it with warm water. Wringing it out, I take it back into the bedroom. Emika is passed out in the middle of the bed, lying on her stomach. Her breathing is still fast, so I know she's not fully asleep yet. With a smile, I rub the cloth between her legs. She whimpers, twitching her hips, but she's so far gone, she doesn't do much else. I chuckle under my breath and lean down to kiss her shoulder.

"Get some rest. I'll be back," I whisper.

"Mm," she hums, not even bothering to open her eyes.

I kiss her cheek because I can't resist how cute she is.

I toss the washcloth into the laundry basket in her bathroom and get dressed as best I can with my torn shirt. Making sure everything is straight and I don't look like I just got fucked, I cover Emika with a blanket before reluctantly leaving the room.

Straightening my shoulders, I change into a new shirt in my room and head back downstairs, following the sound of music and drunken racket to start my plan.

What better way to get people talking than to get them completely wasted?

As I eye the room, a smile curves my lips as I spot my victim.

Five

EMIKA

My room is dark when I wake, but light filters in from my open doorway. Blinking against it, I jump when someone stumbles in, knocking over the end table by the door. The vase shatters on the floor, and I jerk upright.

"Shit." Kade's deep voice fills the room.

I scramble off the bed, cool air hitting my naked body. "Are you okay?"

I turn on a lamp and rush to the sitting chair my robe is draped over in the corner I usually read in. With Kade's size, he's staggering around like a giant fumbling through my room.

"Are you drunk?!" I exclaim.

I've never seen him drink more than a glass or two of sake. Even at the parties my father throws.

"Did you go back downstairs after I fell asleep?"

He laughs, tossing his suit jacket over his shoulder as he comes further into the room and points down at the glass. "I'll get that. Tomorrow. I'm just buzzed. No drunk."

"Seriously?" I cross my arms under my breasts after tying my robe on. "Why would you go back downstairs? You know what they do down there at night."

I sound like a petulant child, but I'm a bit hurt he would go down there instead of lying next to me.

"Was I not enough? Did you have to go find a whore to fuck?"

He waves a hand at me after taking off his tie. He's fumbling with his shirt buttons, so his voice is muffled as he looks down. "I had work to do."

"No one works on nights my father has his 'get-togethers.' Even I'm not that stupid."

Kade growls in frustration as he gets through the buttons and pulls his shirttails from his slacks, tossing his shirt to the floor too. "Not for him. For me."

I scoff. "What work did you need to do for yourself that included getting wasted in a room full of lap-dancing whores?"

"I wasn't fucking anyone. Damn, Emika. Give me some credit. Why would I need them when I have you?" He shakes his head and chuckles like I'm the crazy one.

"What work, Kade?"

Pausing, he looks over at me. "Can't tell you yet."

"When can you tell me?"

"Hopefully soon." He pulls off his shoes and flops back onto the bed. "Now, come over here and sleep with me."

I walk to the bed, still mad. When I'm close enough, he yanks me on top of him. I fall with an oomph onto his hard chest. Immediately, the smell of cheap perfume and liquor fills my senses.

Scoffing, I push off him and get to my feet. "Go back to your room."

He sits up, eyes narrowing at me. "What the hell is your problem?"

"You can't tell me why you were down there drinking, and you smell like every other man in that room. I know yakuza. They think they can do anything they want because they get greedy. I thought you were different, but I see you're not. I can handle a lot of things, Kade, but lying is not one of them."

With a glare, he snaps, "I'm not lying! I went downstairs to work, and that's all you need to know right now."

"Lying and hiding things are the same thing. At least to me, they are. I need more from you if we're going to continue this…whatever it is."

"You're fucking me while being engaged to a psychopath," Kade's words accuse me in his drunken slumber, as if it's important to our current argument. "I'm allowed a few fucking thoughts to myself."

"I didn't choose to marry Kenji— "

"Don't you fucking dare say his name to me!" He shows me a small space between his index finger and thumb. "I'm this close to putting a bullet in his head."

I roll my eyes. "Either way, our situation is different. You know about him. I don't want this life. I don't want to be tied to the criminal world forever. I want to marry someone who loves me and has a real job, but that's not possible."

"It is, if you stay with me."

My eyes widen at the suddenly serious and calm look on his face. "B-but you're a criminal too, and my father— "

"Your father is about to lose everything," Kade cuts me off. "I'm not a criminal, Emika—not originally, anyway—and I can go back to that life anytime. I swear. But I can't tell you the truth yet. I need you to trust me."

He stands and reaches for me, but I step back. The hurt that flashes in his eyes has me wincing.

"I'm sorry. I just can't," I say in a bare whisper as thickness coats my throat. My voice breaks, just like my heart. "Trust without cause is not something I can do anymore. I've learned what happens when I trust people. It only hurts me."

"Baby…"

"Please, just go." I put up my hand and turn away. Holding my head high, I walk toward the bathroom.

"I'm a hitman."

"I know that!"

"For a client in the United States."

The words are so rushed, I almost don't register them. My legs stop moving, and I'm rigid, staring wide-eyed through the bathroom door, but I don't see it. My brain has his words on repeat.

I shake my head vehemently. "I…I don't understand."

The sound of his exhale has tears filling my eyes. "I'm undercover, hired to kill your father for kidnapping."

"What's your name?"

Another exhale. "Not Kade."

I close my eyes and the tears fall. I want to believe he's lying, but his voice is so defeated, I know he's telling the truth. Turning slowly, I look up at him.

With pleading eyes, I ask, "You're here to kill my father?"

His eyes hold a serious and sober look now. They are cold as he looks at me. A killer's eyes. It hurts, but I still need to hear everything. I need to know what's going to happen to us.

To me and him. To me and my family.

I'm not yakuza, but I'm still a bystander. A witness.

He told me the truth, and I can't live with that knowledge. A professional never leaves witnesses.

All the time he was staying with my family, he had a plan in motion. And I was just a toy for him to play with as he worked on finishing my father and my family.

What we share isn't real. Never was. It was just sex. For him.

I'm such a fool for thinking otherwise.

Running a hand over his face, Kade says the thing I'm dreading most. "Not just him."

He used me.

"Why me, then?" I hear myself asking. I need to know. "You never asked me shit, and my father would kill you if he knew you were sleeping with me. Why would you risk everything you're here for?"

He chuckles dryly. "I didn't come to you. You came to me, remember?"

I nod, wiping my tears, and he sighs.

"Emika, I was going to tell you everything when this was over. I guess I had a bit too much to drink. Spouting stupid shit. This is why I don't drink on the job."

"Why tell me at all?" I laugh humorlessly. "I didn't need to know. You're just going to go home when this is over, and I'll be dead somewhere, rotting with the rest of my family."

His jaw tics. "I'm taking you with me. I can cover our tracks like we were never here. Give you a new life. A better one."

My eyes widen. "You kill people! How is that a better life? And I can't abandon my family!"

He stands. "Why not? You said it yourself, you didn't want this life!"

"Maybe not, but I won't turn against them!" I yell. "Yes, they do bad things and my life hasn't been perfect, but I love them. Family always sticks together."

"That's your father's bullshit trying to save his own ass!"

I shake my head. He will not understand. "Family first."

He promises me a new life, a better one where we're together, but at what cost? I'll be living my life with the man who murdered my family. I may not be on good terms with them, and I don't agree with what they've done, but they're all I have. They're still my family.

"Your father has brainwashed you," he says.

"You need to leave." I storm toward the bathroom. "This is over. All of it."

He rushes forward, but I shut and lock the door before he can get to me. I jump, closing my eyes as he bangs on the door and begs me to come out. Sitting in the corner by the shower, I pull my legs to my chest and cover my ears as the tears fall.

He could break down the door. It surprises me that he doesn't. Eventually, the noise stops, and I drop my hands. I hold my breath, quieting my sobs as I listen to his footsteps retreat and the bedroom door closing.

I let go and cry, sobbing for my family. For my love for a man who doesn't exist.

And most of all, I cry in guilt that I will not do anything to save any of us.

Kade may not be who he said he was, but I love him all the same. I cannot betray him by telling my family what is coming, and I cannot betray my family by running away.

Silence is all I have, and silence is all I'll give.

Six

KADE

The sun won't rise for several more hours, but I can't sleep. Instead, I use the time to set my plan into motion.

I take a few aspirin and down them with water to help sober up. After a cold shower, I slip on my black work gloves and sneak into the boss's office, locking the door behind me. Working alone, you must learn various tricks to be as good of a hitman as I am. It takes brains, skill, and a touch of brute force to do what I do.

It also takes a cold heart, but somehow, Emika broke through the ice I've been building around it for over a decade.

Sitting behind the desk, I power on the computer and hack into Ren's email system. Most messages passed between contacts in Japan are done through emails, so it's easy to find the list of names I need. I've done my homework, so I know the name of every permanent staff member inside the house.

Compiling all ten email addresses into one message, I type out a short, but firm letter, telling them all to leave once everyone has retired for the night. No cleaning, and if they say a word to anyone about the message, they will be permanently removed from the payroll and disposed of. With Ren's murderous background, it won't be hard for them to believe he's the one who sent the letters out.

I press send and delete the message from the sent tab. Shutting down the computer, I leave as if I'd never been there.

I head back to my room, listening to the noise downstairs until it dies down and everyone returns to their rooms. After a quick phone call to an old Navy SEAL buddy to make sure he's in place, I'm ready to go, but I give the guests an extra hour to pass out from the festivities in case they decide to have a nightcap with one of the dancers or mistresses. I hate to do it, but I can't save them.

To be honest, the women may not be killers themselves, but they are dirty in their own way. No one will miss them. The dancers will go home, but most mistresses know what's going on in the house and live here permanently. Again, nothing I can do except make their deaths quick and painless. If I send them a letter too, they'll start talking against the orders of the message and ruin my entire plan.

When I hear the last bit of movement die to nothingness, I wait another ten minutes and then use the recording I have of Emika's wasted brother spilling the beans on the human trafficking to find where the teens are held. Sneaking out, I get into one of the boss's empty cargo vans and head to the location. It's actually the dumbest place, in my opinion.

When I pull up to the ritzy house, I notice the nameplate on the siding.

Fuck. I should have known they'd use one of the members' houses. What would they have done when Emika moved in with Kenji? Moved the girls or left them for her to find?

I shake my head as I pick the lock on the door and go inside. There's no alarm system or guards. They really are full of themselves, thinking no one will find out or break in. Like they're such badasses no one would dare cross them. I roll my eyes as I find a door leading down into a basement.

Turning on the flashlight, I hold it over my gun as I creep down the stairs. I don't want any surprises, and it's always better to be cautious in these situations.

At the bottom, my light scans over futons with disturbed blankets, showing people were on them recently. The smell in the room is musty from lack of airflow and feces. I find at least two dozen bedding sets around the small space smashed together on the floor, but it isn't until I reach the far corner that I see the girls huddled together.

The breath I hadn't known I was holding rushes out. "I'm here to take you home."

No one moves. They just stare at me like they've been tricked before and don't believe me.

Probably the way they all ended up here. Tricked and taken advantage of.

I'm not good at hostage situations, especially with young girls. I'm a killer by instinct. I have no words of gentleness or smooth manipulation for the poor girls. It makes convincing them to leave with me that much harder.

Still, I try. "I'm here to save you. You'll be safe. I promise."

I'm not sure it helps, but time is ticking, and I hold my

breath while I wait for something to happen.

Finally, one stands. She coaxes the others to follow, and I can breathe again. With a guiding hand, I point toward the way I came and whisper instructions. I'm not leaving this room until everyone is out.

After the last girl exits, I move to the front of the group and help them into the van.

I'm restless on the drive to meet up with my contact. There's always a chance that things could go sideways. I mean, I have a van full of teenage girls hiding in the back with barely a scrap of clothing on. Not only do I have to worry about the yakuza catching on, but also the police. It won't be an easy thing to explain away.

Luckily, we make it to the private airport unscathed in two hours. Going through a city airport will raise questions. It took time to find a place that won't ask questions and be mostly deserted for us to move the girls. It also helps to toss around some cash, which my buddy did for me in advance. I'll have to wire the money back, plus more for his help, after this is over.

We don't waste time talking. A simple chin lift in greeting as we file the girls on his plane is all we exchange. In under ten minutes, they're up in the air and I'm headed back to Emika's.

One job done. Now to finish off the rest.

This is the hard part. I don't want to hurt Emika, and I don't understand her loyalty to her family, but I guess family is family whether they're good or bad. Even if they are cruel and control everything in her life without a care for her happiness, she still loves them. My contract states I'm supposed to kill everyone involved. I was fine with that until I fell in love with Emika.

The thought of hurting her has my chest tightening. And

if I can, I'd like to keep her from hating me. The only way to do that is to let her family live. But I can't let my client know they survived, or my name will be dragged through the dirt. I have a clean track record when it comes to my job. I'm going to have to think of every possible scenario and cover all loose ends to keep my status.

The ride gives me plenty of time to come up with a new plan that will hopefully satisfy everyone. I've still got an hour before sunrise when I get back.

God help me. I'm going to do something I never have before.

But love doesn't let you choose. It just happens and you go for the ride. That's exactly what I'm doing.

I can't kill Emika. I won't. She can either come with me or take what she can and run the other way.

Taking a deep breath, I strap up, making sure I have enough ammo and step out of the van. I leave it by the garage out of the way. I have another car waiting out front, which I'll be using after I'm done. It's already packed and ready to go.

Here goes nothing.

I didn't lock the door when I left, so I stroll inside and shut off any lingering emotions, pushing all thoughts of Emika to the back of my mind. I start on the bottom floor and enter the two bedrooms there. Using pillows and a suppressor on the barrel of my gun, I place it over each person's sleeping face and pull the trigger. The suppressor is not quiet. Nothing like in the movies. It barely hides any sound, but no one stirs from the noise, too wasted from the party. I'm surprised, but not completely unhappy about it.

The only downside is that it takes me longer to get to everyone this way.

I don't feel anything as I move from room to room, ending enough lives to empty more than one clip.

I know Emika must hear me. She's the only sober person here, but there's no movement or lights coming from her room.

I pause outside her father's bedroom and stare up at the ceiling. It's almost over. Just a few more loose ends to tie up. What no one knows won't hurt them.

Right?

I pull myself together. A nosy neighbor will have heard all those shots and called the cops. There is no time to hesitate.

Rolling my shoulders, I go into the bedroom and look down at Emika's stepmother and father, both sleeping soundly.

Seven

EMIKA

I stand by the window and stare out. Each time I hear the gun go off, I jerk, tears streaming silently down my face. I'm already dressed. I'd rather not die naked, and after what Kade did to me, he doesn't deserve to see my bare skin. I know he'll come here.

No witnesses. That's the motto of any criminal.

But he'll have to look me in the eyes when he shoots me. I won't cower or beg him to change his mind. I've accepted my fate, much like I've done my entire life since moving here. I force my tears to dry up when the shooting has stopped for longer than a few seconds.

It's my turn.

I hear the door to my room opening and slowly turn to face him. I know I must look like a mess, eyes red and swollen, but

I don't care. There's no reason to impress him anymore. I hold my head high and straighten my spine. He studies me, and I see his eyes flash with sadness before it's gone again.

He nods and glances down. "I guess this is goodbye."

I don't reply. I don't think I can even if I try, so I say nothing. My heart twists in pain, breaking at the sight of him.

He clears his throat and motions behind him. "I can't say I regret anything, because it brought me here to you." He inhales. "This is your chance at a new beginning. Don't waste it. I love you, Emika."

He turns and walks out.

I'm so confused. Is he just going to leave me here, among the dead bodies? I have nowhere to go. That's when I realize I don't want to be without him. He may be a criminal and he may have taken everything from me, but the thought of losing him is far worse than losing my family.

Does that make me a bad person? Probably. But I haven't been raised by good people. There's sure to be some evil in me as well. And if that means I can be with the man I love, who cares?

He never judges me, and he said last night he'd take me with him. I open my mouth to call after him, but close it as my father's voice booms from down the hall.

"Get your sister, you idiot! We must hurry!"

Eight

KADE

Ren's rustling around in his office as I walk past. He's got a stash of cash for emergencies hidden in that office. I've seen him adding to it. He probably has aliases and fake IDs for everyone as well.

Emika's brother sees me as he comes out of the office doorway and stalls for a moment, eyeing me. I wait to see what he does. I'm not afraid. I'd like nothing more than an excuse to blow his brains out, but apparently, he's smarter than I thought. He shoulders past me to get to Emika. I continue on my way.

It hurts like hell that she didn't choose me. I could see it in her determined stance as she looked at me when I entered her room.

She's made her choice. And I'm not it.

Am I disappointed? Hell yeah. But I understand. I came to kill her family. To kill everyone she's ever known.

I'm a criminal. She deserves more, and I've made sure she has that chance. No one will ever try to force her to do anything she doesn't want to anymore.

She's free.

After the threat I've given her father, none of them will be showing their faces in the underworld for a while. If Ren's smart, he'll never do it again. He can live a straightlaced life, or I'll come back to hunt him down. He and his son won't live next time. They know it. I know it. Hopefully, their fear is greater than their greed.

I've just reached the stairs when I hear her voice.

"You let my family live?"

I turn in time to see her stop running down the hall and come to a halt in front of me. "With conditions, yes."

"And the girls?"

"Safely on their way home."

"Thank you," Emika whispers as tears fill her eyes. "They are not innocent people, but they are all I have."

"I know." I reach out and wipe a tear that falls down her cheek. "Be happy and free, Emi."

Unable to keep looking at her, I let my hand drop and head downstairs. I don't look back. I can't. I'll beg her to come with me if I do, and that's not what she needs. I hear her footsteps rush away from me. It hurts like hell. I've been through some fucked-up shit, but this is the worst pain I've ever experienced.

Keeping my head up, I focus on what I need to do. Emika will be okay. Her father will whisk her, his son, and his wife away to hide until the heat dies down. As I head to the rental I have waiting outside, I hear several pounding feet following.

I open the driver's door and watch the Morihei family rush into a taxi that pulls up. Emika is corralled by her father into the car after her stepmother before Ren climbs in. Her brother takes the front seat. She doesn't have much of a chance to do anything, but follow orders as the cab drives off.

Police sirens echo in the distance, signaling it's time to blow this joint. I slide into the driver's seat of the sleek ride I've picked for just this occasion and turn over the engine. The purr has a calming effect on me. I set charges around the house weeks ago in preparation for this moment. Placing the detonator in my lap, I put the car in gear and ride into the street.

The sight of Emika standing in the road has me slamming on my brakes. She wastes no time jumping into the passenger side. I stare at her in bewilderment. Her eyes are still red and teary, but there's a gleam in the dark depths that give me hope.

Hope for our future together.

I try to get my mind to work and say something, but I can do nothing except watch her.

A slow smile curves her lips. "Should we go, or..."

Shaking off my shock, I say, "You're sure?"

The smile she gives me takes my breath away. "You let my family live, for me. Now I want to live for myself. With you."

The sirens grow louder, catching my attention. Glancing in my rearview mirror, I can see their lights flashing as they get closer.

"Seatbelt," I say.

She's barely buckled in before I'm peeling out of there. I hold the detonator out to her. She smirks as she clicks it. I turn the corner as the car rocks with the waves of the explosion that takes over her childhood home.

"Can we go to America, Kade?" Emika asks with childlike wonder. "I have my fake passport and ID."

She holds them up, making me laugh.

"We can go wherever you want, but there's something you should know."

"What?"

"My name's Dane."

"I don't hate it." Emika unbuckles her seatbelt and leans over to wrap her arms around my neck. "But it may take a few spankings to memorize it."

"God, I hope so."

Also by Maureen Shigeno

SWEET AND SASSY DUET

1. *Corrupting Sweetness*
2. *Claiming Sassy* (Coming Soon!)

WHIMSICAL COVE REVAMPED SERIES

1. *Cove*
2. *Crave* (Coming Soon!)
3. *Chaos* (Coming Soon!)

STANDALONES

1. *Criminally Bound*
2. *Fate Laced Kiss*
3. *My Pact With Santa*
4. *A Need for Darkness*
5. *Merging His Assets*
6. *Fighting For Harmony*
7. *Stealing My Sister's Mate*

MAUREEN SHIGENO
love. passion. heat.

Maureen Shigeno is a romance author. She writes in a variety of sub-genres and loves **HEA** endings. She is happily married with two kids. Her passions include reading, writing, spending time with her family, and cooking.

If you would like to be kept up-to-date on upcoming novels by Maureen Shigeno, or join in on any of the fun we share, please scan the code below.

KEEP IN TOUCH